For my Birdie, Charlie

The illustrations for this book were done in watercolor and collage on watercolor paper
The text and display type were set in Horley Old Style • Book design by Liz Casal

Copyright © 2011 by Sujean Rim • All rights reserved. Except as permitted under the U.S. Copyright Act of 1976, no part of this publication may be reproduced, distributed, or transmitted in any form or by any means, or stored in a database or retrieval system, without the prior written permission of the publisher. • Little, Brown and Company • Hachette Book Group • 237 Park Avenue, New York, NY 10017 • Visit our website at www.lb-kids.com • Little, Brown and Company is a division of Hachette Book Group, Inc. • The Little, Brown name and logo are trademarks of Hachette Book Group, Inc • The publisher is not responsible for websites (or their content) that are not owned by the publisher. • First Edition: September 2011 • Library of Congress Cataloging-in-Publication Data • Rim, Sujean. • Birdie's big-girl dress / by Sujean Rim. — 1st ed. • p. cm. • Summary: Birdie's excitement over her approaching birthday party fades when she finds that her favorite party dress is too small, and nothing at her mother's favorite boutique is quite right. • ISBN 978-0-316-13287-9 • [1. Clothing and dress—Fiction. 2. Birthdays—Fiction. 3. Parties—Fiction.] I. Title. • PZ7.R4575Bik 2011 • [E]—dc22 • 2010049435 • 10 9 8 7 6 5 4 3 2 1 • SC • Printed in China

BIRDIE'S BIG-GIRL DRESS

SUJEAN RIM

Little, Brown and Company
New York Boston

Birdie and her mother were busy.

Tomorrow was Birdie's birthday party.

And tomorrow was almost here!

Birdie skipped around the house with her dog, Monster, as she finished the party decorations. She couldn't wait to dance to her favorite songs, play her favorite games, and share birthday cake with all her friends!

Birdie went to get her very favorite party dress from her closet. But when she tried to put it on . . . it was too small!

"Don't worry, sweetheart," said Mommy.
"We'll go shopping tomorrow and get
you something that will fit just right."

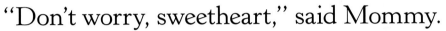

That night, Birdie dreamed of dresses—

fluttery floral sundresses . . . lovely lace sheaths . . . chic chiffon gowns. . . .

The next morning, Birdie, Mommy, and Monster walked to their favorite boutique.

Guess who was there — Birdie's friends Coco, Charlie, and Eve!

"Hi, Birdie!" said Coco. "Look at the dress I'm getting for your party!"

"And look at mine!" added Eve.

"Ooh!" squealed Birdie. "They're perfect."

Birdie's mother handed her a
fabulously frilly sundress.

It was beautiful — but it was
too big to play games in.

Next Birdie tried on a lacy sheath.
It was silky and smooth — but it
was too snug to eat cake in.

So Birdie reached for a gauzy gown.
It made Birdie feel like a lady — but it
was too long to dance in.

Birdie tried on dress after dress,
but none of them felt just like her.

Poor Birdie. She had nothing to wear to her own party.

"What are you going to do now?" asked Charlie.

"I don't know. . . . But I'll think of something," she said. "See you at the party!" Birdie took her mommy's hand as they went home.

When they got back, Birdie had an idea. "Mommy?" Birdie asked. "Can Monster and I go up to the attic? Maybe there's something special there—just for me and my birthday."

"Okay, darling," Mommy said with a smile. "Don't be too long."

"Oh!" exclaimed Birdie when she turned on the light.

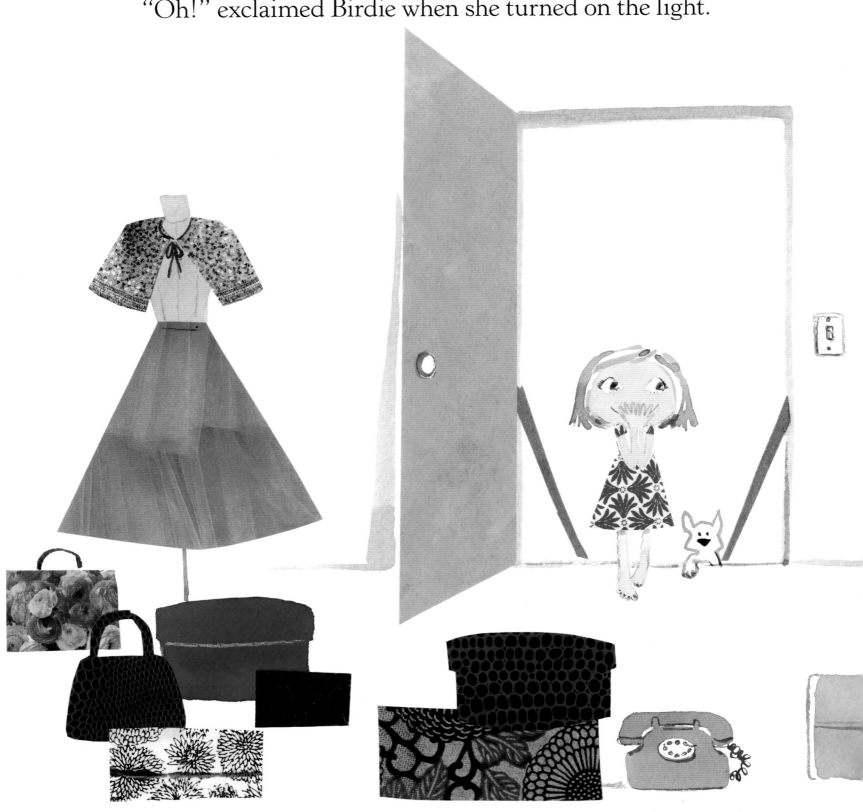

The attic was a **magical place.**

Birdie giggled as she wrapped a big shawl around herself.
She felt so . . . *stylish!*

"Here, Monster, try on this top hat."
Monster felt so . . . *dapper!*

But whose clothes were these?
Birdie knew they must have belonged
to her grandma and grandpa.

"Ooh, look, Monster! Isn't this the most beautiful dress?"
Monster looked pretty in pink, too.

"I love Grandpa's fancy vest!"

"Ooh . . . such pretty hats—this one is my very favorite!"
Before Birdie knew it, she was ready for her party!
And just in time.

Ding-dong! Ding-dong!

The doorbell rang and rang—Coco and Charlie and Eve were here!

"Wow, Birdie! You look beautiful. I haven't seen those clothes in ages," Mommy said.

"Oooh...aaah!" her friends squealed. "Is that your new dress?"

"Yes," said Birdie with a smile.
She looked down and twirled.

"It's my new Birdie dress!"

"Happy birthday, Birdie!"
everyone sang.
And it was!